To Mungo Taylor who would never be naughty like Mr Davies

First published 1996 by
Walker Books Ltd
87 Vauxhall Walk
London SE11 5HJ

10 9 8 7 6 5 4 3 2 1

Printed in Hong Kong

British Library Cataloguing in Publication Data.
A catalogue record for this book
is available from the British Library.

ISBN 0-7445-2525-X

Mr Davies
and the Baby

Charlotte
Voake

WALKER BOOKS
AND SUBSIDIARIES
LONDON • BOSTON • SYDNEY

ONCE upon a time there was a little dog called Mr Davies. All day long he stayed in his garden.

He sniffed the smells and dug holes in the flower beds.

He ate his meals,
and when it rained he

slept in his kennel.

Next door to Mr Davies

lived a baby.

Every single day, the baby and his mother went out for a walk.

"Hello, Mr Davies," the baby's mother said. The baby clapped his hands and laughed and Mr Davies wagged his tail. Mr Davies watched them go down the road and wished he could go with them.

Then one day,
Mr Davies found he
could squeeze
right under
the gate,
and he
came out
to meet
the baby.

The baby was very excited. So was Mr Davies, and he jumped about and wagged his tail. "Nice dog," said the baby's mother. "Now go home, Mr Davies."

But Mr Davies was much
too excited to listen.
He just wagged his
tail harder
and followed
them down
the road.

Mr Davies was very good until he saw some ducks.

"Mr Davies, come here!" shouted the baby's mother.

The next day
Mr Davies went
for a walk
with the
baby
again.
But this
time he
chased
a cat.

WOOF!

And the next day Mr Davies saw a man on a bicycle and chased him up the road.

People asked the baby's mother,"Is this your dog?" "No,he is not," she said.

One day the baby's mother
went next door.

"Please could you stop
Mr Davies getting out of the
garden?" she asked.

The next day Mr Davies ran to meet the baby

and the baby held out
his arms . . .

But just as Mr Davies got
to the gate he came
to a sudden
STOP.

Poor Mr Davies had
been tied to his kennel!

He barked
and barked

but he could not get free.

The baby and his mother set off down the road. Soon they couldn't hear Mr Davies barking any more. The baby was sad. Even the baby's mother was sorry that Mr Davies had been tied up.

It was very quiet.

Then suddenly they heard a SMASHING and a BANGING and a happy BARKING coming towards them. It was Mr Davies...

and he was bringing